THE DALAI LAMA

MESSAGE

This book by Alan Clements inspires people, young and old. He addresses the reality that life can be fraught with difficulties and yet full of joy. If you have compassion and wisdom, it's always possible to overcome whatever challenges you face. I admire Alan's determination to pass this important message on to the next generation — keeping his daughter especially in mind.

With my prayers,

January 3, 2022

Published in 2022 by World Dharma Publications
© Alan Clements 1997, 2008, 2012, 2020, 2022

Library of Congress Cataloging-in-Publication Data
Clements, Alan 1951 —
Tonight I Met a Deva, An Angel of Love

p. cm.
ISBN 978-1-953508-24-9

1. Children 2. Buddhism—Meditation—Mindfulness 3. Educational 4. Liberty—Freedom
—Buddhism 5. Spiritual life—Buddhism—Non-sectarian 6. Human rights—All aspects
7. Social, Political and Environmental Justice—All 8. Activism—All
9. Consciousness—All 10. Politics—Global 11. Body, Mind and Spirit

First printing, February 28, 2022
ISBN 978-1-953508-24-9

Artwork by Soyolmaa Davaakhuu (pages; cover, 13, 14, 25, 31, 32-33, 44-45, 47, 50-51, 52-53),
Tilly Campbell Allen (pages; 3, 9, 20, 34, 38, 59, 60), Kali Levitov (pages; 19, 22, 42-43, 48),
Kay Konrad (pages; 6, 10-11, 16-17, 26-27, 28, 37, 40, 56).

Layout and typesetting by Justine Elliott · Design Lasso.

World Dharma Publications
www.WorldDharma.com

THIS BOOK IS DEDICATED TO

My beloved daughter, Sahra Bella.

You are Amazing.
And to children
in All countries, all over the world.

And equally, to the child that lies
in the heart of every Adult.

And to the almost-born children everywhere,
in All dimensions of our sacred Universe—

Returning into Life at this very moment.

"Your Vision will only become clear when
you can look into your own heart.

Who looks outside, dreams;
who looks inside, Awakens."

—CARL GUSTAV JUNG

"We are star stuff which has taken
its destiny into its own hands."

—CARL SAGAN

tonight i met a deva
an Angel of Love

I was all **Alone** in my room tonight,
When suddenly appeared a wondrous light!
I was **Astonished**! 'Twas so brilliant! So bright!
Never had I seen such a radiant sight!

I felt a presence, as my eyes opened wide.
Then an **Angel** appeared right by my side.
Her skin was aglow with a luminous hue,
Transparent and glistening like droplets of dew.

My heart started to open into this vast space,
And all my thoughts vanished,
Except **Love**, **Peace**, and **Grace**.

The **Angel** spoke as I trembled and stared,
Her words were gentle, they flowed like a prayer.

She called herself **Deva—an Angel of Love**.
She spoke of her home, in a realm high above.
She described a place, heavenly and pure,
Where love and beauty playfully endure.

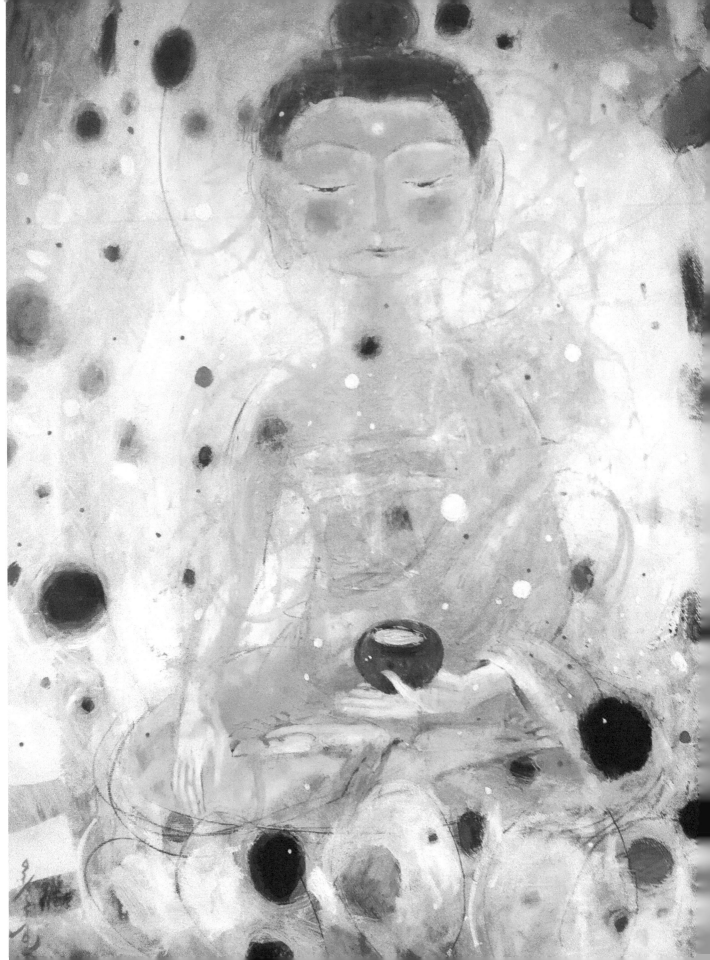

"**All Beings** in this land live in radiant illumination,
And speak from the heart, in psychic communication.
Bejeweled castles glimmer amongst crystalline trees,
Transparent waters fill calm tranquil seas.

This realm's called **Tusita**, where day never falls to night,
Here even one thought brings the heart's delight.
This Mystical land, which **Maitreya** calls home,
Is where this **Buddha**-to-be sits on a throne.

In this magical realm, beyond where eagles fly,
Nothing lasts forever; All life must die.

But don't be alarmed, there's no need to fear!
Death's not the end!" she whispered in my ear.
"**Maitreya**—the coming **Buddha**—will soon take rebirth,

And this **Bodhisattva** will return to Earth!"

"But why is he returning, dear **Deva**?" I asked.

"To bring True Freedom," said she. "At long last.
To share Love and Compassion, as vast as an ocean,
With those seeking goodness, with mindful devotion.
To bring Great **Dharma** Awakening, to all who can see,
Teaching **Four Noble Truths**, setting humankind free!"

"Oh **Deva**," I sighed, "can you help me understand?"

"Yes of course," she smiled gently, And gave me her hand.

"The First Noble Truth is that Humans are ensnared,
 By a fearsome condition, known as **Dukkha**, or despair.
 This suffering takes roots from within our own mind,

And if unseen, keeps us trapped and firmly entwined.
 Known simply as greed, ignorance, hatred and fear,
 Their roots begin inside, just... right here.
 Hatred hurts you, and it also hurts me;

It keeps us All from being free.
 Greed tries to control Life's natural flow,
 And this grasping and clinging **we must see—and let go**!

These states are like **Actors**, running on scripts;

They're known as ego—or mind masks—all playing their tricks.

Our lives are like **dream stories**, movies on a screen,

And we are just actors, scene by scene.

My dear," **Deva** said gently, "Remove the mask.

Beautifying the mind is the MOST noble human task."

I whispered to the **Deva**, "I'd like to be free.
But how? And... why?

And does it even matter, if I'm only going to die?

If life is just a dream, and will all soon end,
Shouldn't I enjoy it? Can't I just pretend?"

Deva just smiled, then shook her head to allay:
"Oh, dear child, it works in such a different way.

The Law of Cause and Effect simply means
Our **Actions** follow us—and stay;
Like a shadow chasing us around all day
The Law of **Karma** never goes away.

Your **Actions** are seeds growing your life on Earth;
Shaping everything you do, and then your rebirth.
Bitter seeds grow bitter fruit;
Bad seeds grow bad fruit.
What you sow, you then must reap.

So, I urge you Dear One, plant only **seeds of love**,
And I promise you, in peace you will sleep."

Kay Konrad

So, I dug my hands into the soil

Which **Appeared** before my eyes,

Creating my special field;
Sowing only seeds of Beauty,
That I hope will rise high to the skies.

"Now the Second Noble Truth," the **Deva** declared,
"Is kind of like subtraction.
As we **remove** craving from inside our mind,
We lessen the causes of dissatisfaction.
'I want this', 'now that', 'now here', 'now there',
Pleasures fleeting, never enough, 'I want more!' I declare."

"So how to be free?" cried I. "Please, please show me the way!"
"The problem," she answered, "are our habits in life.
These blindly cause **Dukkha** bringing suffering and strife.

We must navigate each day, with mindful grace.
Letting things move freely, creating life from this space.
And with the mask off," **Deva** laughed,

"Soon you will know your real, true face.
It's great fun, designing your very own **Karma**.
We call this **The Art of living the Dharma**."

"How cool is that!" said I, and **Deva** just had to laugh.
"It's true," she said chuckling "But come!
I'll show you more of the Path."

The **Deva** then shared the Third Noble Truth: **Liberation**,
True release from suffering, pain and separation.

"This state's called **Nibbana**, where the heart is at Peace,
Here there's No desire, No grasping, No Regret or Grief.
Where everything you might cling to, you SEE and release,
And every single burden is replaced with Perfect Peace.

And now," the **Deva** said, "to find this place of Liberation,
I'll show you the map to find your salvation."

She then quietly unfurled a lotus flower in her hand.
"Eight petals. Eight steps. **Are you sure you are ready?**"
My answer was "Yes!" And so we began...

"The lotus is a sacred map," **Deva** leaned in intently to say.
"If you want to find **Nibbana**, you must walk the Middle Way."
So, we stepped into the magic flower, petals one and two.

"The first was **Understanding**.
Pure Thoughts were number two.
These petals shape our minds,
Next will come our lives, removing everything untrue."

"To **speak**, **Act**, and **live without blame**, are petals three to five.
These ask our words and actions to be nothing but divine,
Harmonious and loving—without harm of any kind."

We stepped into the sixth and seventh
petals: **Illumination**

Through practice of Right Effort and
Mindful Consideration;

Until we reached **Concentration**, the
eighth and final step to peace,

Where the mind becomes very focused,
and graspings simply cease.

"And now," said the **Deva**, "Do not be swept away!
  You've reached the final step. Don't falter! Don't sway!

Feelings are like bubbles: In time they all just fly.

  And thoughts will come and go, like clouds drifting by.
  Let them pass, control your mind, but with ease, like a dance!
  The path to **Nibbana** will guide you, and will certainly enhance!
  The eight-petaled lotus reminds both elders and youth,
  Of this great map to peace—the fourth and final **Noble Truth**."

Then the **Deva** fell silent. Was her teaching now complete?
She began again softly, "I have one more thing to show:
It's the **most** important Truth you'll ever come to know…"

And then she paused, and my attention was caught:
She said, "The one who goes seeking…is the one who is sought."
In silence we paused. "So… I am the one?"
"Yes, darling child it's you!
Nibbana's essence is intuition—it's your own inner guide—
And the very best way to stay true!"

Deva began to glow and glisten, radiating pure love and light.
I could scarcely behold her, she was blinding my sight!

My eyelids grew heavy, slowly closed, and I yawned.
And when my eyes reopened, **Angel-Deva** was ... gone.

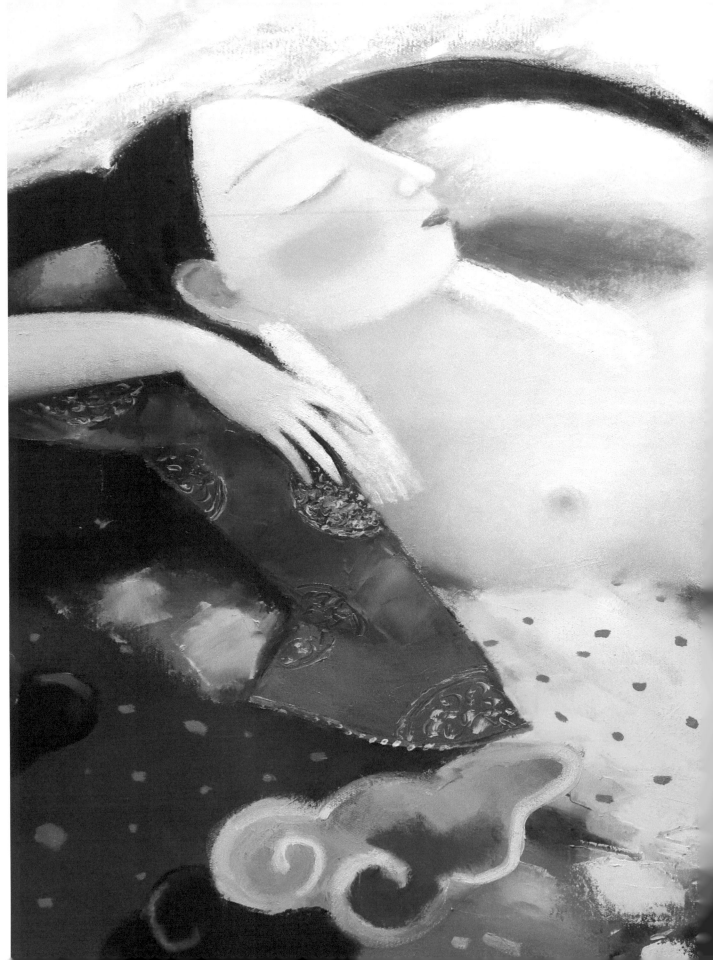

Now I rest here, **Awe-struck**.
What a vision. What a night!

I was so blessed to meet a **Deva**—
and receive her Gift of Inner Sight.

And as I absorb this great wonder,
and drift off again to sleep.

I dream of the **Dharma**, this
treasure, that I hold so very deep.

And now, I have come to know the truth:
Only **love** can ever remain.

Tonight I met a **Deva**
And I am, nevermore, the same.

GLOSSARY OF TERMS

Deva: In Buddhism *Devas* are highly evolved beings who inhabit celestial dimensions of existence. As beings primarily of light, their lifespans are considerably longer than humans. *Devas* are associated with great beauty, wisdom, and love.

Tusita: Refers to one of the six celestial (or *Deva*) realms of existence, and is reachable through advanced meditative attainments. It is where the *Bodhisattva Maitreya* resides, before being reborn on Earth as the next *Buddha*.

Bodhisattva: Refers to an individual who has made a resolution to become a *Buddha*—a fully awakened Being—dedicated to developing the ten qualities of *Buddhahood*: (1) generosity (2) morality (3) renunciation (4) wisdom (5) energy (6) patience (7) truthfulness (8) resolution (9) loving-kindness and (10) equanimity. In turn, a *Bodhisattva*, motivated by compassion, is dedicated to helping others Awaken to the *Dharma* through the Four Noble Truths.

Maitreya: Is the name of the future *Buddha*, presently a *Bodhisattva*—a *Buddha*-to-be—residing in *Tusita*. After his life span as a *Deva*, he will take rebirth on Earth to teach anew the *Dharma*—or law—comprising of the Four Noble Truths. The name *Maitreya* means 'friendliness.'

Buddha: Is one who has perfected the ten attributes of *Buddhahood* (listed above) and achieved *Nibbana*—the complete overcoming of greed, hatred and delusion. Thus, the term *Buddha* literally means Enlightened One, a knower of liberation.

Dharma: Refers to the inherent nature of reality, or the cosmic law underlying right behavior. The *Dharma*, or the nature of reality, is regarded as a universal truth taught by the *Buddha*.

Dukkha: Refers to unpleasant human experiences, causing suffering, pain, sadness, sorrow, distress, grief or misery. It is said that one who is Enlightened (in the Buddhist tradition) has overcome all forms of inner-suffering, originating from hatred, greed and ignorance. Thus, the overcoming of *Dukkha*.

Karma: Means action or deeds. It refers to the principle of cause and effect—of what you sow, you will reap. Or that of bringing upon oneself inevitable results of good or bad, either in this life or in future lives.

Nibbana: Is considered the loftiest of goals in Buddhism and the highest state of consciousness, in which, the individual, through her and his own effort, develops inner-sight or intuitive wisdom, and completely and irreversibly overcomes the forces of hatred, greed and delusion, thus attaining the Third Noble Truth: Liberation from *Dukkha*.

acknowledgements

I'm honored to express my heartfelt gratitude to the beautiful minds that made this book a reality. Without them it would not have been possible to bring this work to the world, to the children, to the not yet born. First out I am who I am, through the Dharma teachings attributed to the Buddha, 2,600 years ago. A deep bow to this man and his wife and child and parents and the honorable Sanghas—the community of nuns and monks and practitioners—over the centuries, to this very day—carrying forward the timeless Dharma teachings of liberation, namely the Four Noble Truths, and the living essence of this book.

A humble bow of love and gratitude to my Dharma teachers, Mahasi Sayadaw of Burma, and his successor, Venerable Sayadaw U Pandita. To the great people of Burma—my Dharma home and family—who provided shelter, medicines, food, robes, and inspiration both as a monk and layperson. I am forever indebted. And equally, I salute the heroic freedom fighters in Myanmar today, many of whom are imprisoned, others dead, showing us—the world—the power of conscience, dignity and moral courage in Action—keeping alive the flame of freedom and universal human rights and the revolutionary unwillingness to cower to fear, tyranny and dictatorship.

A graceful transcendent hug to my beloved Mother and Father, forever in my heart, in this life and onward. To my beloved friends providing for me during this most challenging period of my life, in particular Jenny Chartoff (and our dear Bob, too), along with Matthew Marshall and Grif Griffis, who gifted me with a Dharma Temple to live, create and thrive in over the past two years, while crafting this sacred story.

To the precious souls so near and dear to me, especially Justine Elliott, Kerry Wright, Heidi Gold, Fergus Harlow, and Summer Richardson, who put their Bodhisattva spirits and creative hands onto every page of this book. And equally, the Dharma grace and inspiring conversations offered by my beloveds Jeannine Davies, Catherine de Rham, and Mitch Davidowitz throughout the process, and a few other sacred hearts as well. And to my precious daughter, Sahra Bella Clements Earl, for the inspiration that you are, and the very reason why I wrote this book—For You Precious One.

My deepest gratitude goes to the most amazing artists, Soyolmaa Davaakhuu, Tilly Campbell-Allen, Kali Levitov and Kay Konrad whose majestic paintings grace both the pages and celestial spirit of this book. It took trust and patient flow to enter the most magical serendipity enabling us to meet from around the globe, but it happened. My appreciation for your mastery and magic and the Gift of your generous hearts. Thank you.

A bow of gratitude to Michael Ash and Kali Watanabe, the owners of Dakini As Art, who represent these fine artists to the world. Thank you both for your grace and generosity throughout the entire creative process. So deeply appreciated.

To His Holiness the Dalai Lama for his generous endorsement gracing the cover of this book, and equally to the many other generous souls who offered their own amazing words of support for *Tonight I Met a Deva, an Angel of Love*.

From my heart to yours, blaze on with fearless love.

ALAN E. CLEMENTS
February 28, 2022

about the author

Alan Clements—author, performing artist, and activist—is one of the first Westerners to ordain as a Buddhist monk in the country of Burma, also known as Myanmar, where he trained for nearly four years in Buddhist Psychology and Mindfulness Meditation under the guidance of the late Venerable Mahasi Sayadaw and his successor, the late Venerable Sayadaw U Pandita. After leaving the monastic life, Alan founded World Dharma; a non-sectarian community adhering to the fusion of Eastern and Western wisdom with activism and creative expression. Alan also performs, "Spiritually Incorrect"—an improvisational spoken word show—at theaters worldwide to raise awareness of prisoners of conscience. Alan is also an acclaimed author of numerous books, including The Voice of Hope—Conversations with Burma's (imprisoned) Nobel Peace Laureate, Aung San Suu Kyi, Wisdom For The World: Conversations with Sayadaw U Pandita, Instinct For Freedom, A Future To Believe In, Burma's Voices of Freedom, co-authored with Fergus Harlow, and A Practical Guide to World Dharma and the Practice of Mindful Intelligence—A Video Book. Alan's podcast, "As I See It," is distributed on Apple, YouTube and SoundCloud. For more information, please visit: AlanClements.com.

about the illustrators

The Mongolian artist **Soyolmaa Davaakhuu** was born the third daughter of artist parents in 1977. She grew up in Mongolia's capital city, Ulaanbaatar, and studied art at the University of Culture and Art, Ulaanbaatar from 1995 to 1998. In 2001 she become a member of the Union of Mongolian Artists, the most prestigious art society in the country. Since then she has had a number of solo and collaborative exhibitions in both Mongolian and overseas prestigious s in such countries as the USA, Canada, South Korea, Vietnam and the UK. Her work, from traditional to surreal, is always transformative, exploring themes of dreaming and awakening, the hidden and revealed, and more often than not, celebrates enlightenment manifesting in feminine form.

Tilly Campbell-Allen is a mother, grandmother, artist, and philosophical muser. Half French, half British, born in London. Named Natasha at birth, she comes from a matriarchal lineage of occult thinkers and conscious dietitians. She was first introduced to Buddhism when the family's London home became home to the most venerable Geshe Namgyal Wangchen upon his arrival to the UK, and who 'pet named' her Tilly. The focus of her work finds inspiration from spirituality, quantum mechanics, the natural world, natural health, mythology, and neurology and its implications on our wellbeing.

Kali Levitov is a multi-faceted creator who embraces Thangka painting as a method of creating pathways for liberating feminine awareness across all the world's traditions. Her work as a healer and artist emerge from stillness and deep listening. She enjoys the art of collaboration and the joy and mystery that emerges in the infinite trinity. Most of the images chosen for this book were collaborations with musician and artist Scott Pridgen.

At a young age, **Kay Konrad** hitchhiked through Europe with an aquarelle box and colored pencils to find out what to do with this life. After one year he noticed that painting would be his way of life. In 1985, he got a little book of the Dalai Lama, "Ways of Universal Responsibility". A small drawing of White Tara touched his heart. Soon after he painted a picture of her residing in front of a cave in La Gomera where he lived at that time. The same year he took refuge in the Dharma of Tibetan Buddhism. He has studied with several great masters, including Tenga Rinpoche and Namkhai Norbu Rinpoche. In 1994, he studied traditional Tibetan Thangka painting with Andy Weber. Since then, Thangka painting has become an essential part of his artwork.

To learn more about these artists visit **Dakini As Art**, www.dakiniasart.org

CPSIA information can be obtained
at www.ICGtesting.com
Printed in the USA
LVHW072133250522
719743LV00002B/22